ABCDEF
GHIJKL
MNOPQR
STUVW
XYZ

For Rosie —E.C.

*For my dear mom, Yoonhee, the quiet shining star I always look
up to before I set my foot forward —H.J.*

Henry Holt and Company, *Publishers since 1866*

Henry Holt® is a registered trademark of Macmillan Publishing Group, LLC.

120 Broadway, New York, New York 10271

mackids.com

Text copyright © 2022 by Emily Calandrelli

Illustrations copyright © 2022 by Honee Jang

Library of Congress Cataloging-in-Publication Data is available

ISBN 978-1-250-79734-6

Our books may be purchased in bulk for promotional, educational, or business use. Please contact your local bookseller or the Macmillan Corporate and Premium Sales Department at (800) 221-7945 ext. 5442 or by email at MacmillanSpecialMarkets@macmillan.com.

First edition, 2022

Art was created using Adobe Photoshop

Printed in China by Hung Hing Off-set Printing Co. Ltd., Heshan City, Guangdong Province

1 3 5 7 9 10 8 6 4 2

REACH for the STARS

By Emily Calandrelli

Illustrated by Honee Jang

GODWINBOOKS

Henry Holt and Company
New York

I watch you reach for twirling stars
as I peek in your door.
I stand and wonder what you'll learn
when you can reach for more.

When you wake, you stretch and stretch
with arms up overhead.
You reach for bottles and for thumbs
and blocks and cars and threads.

When you're sad, you reach for me.
I'll hold you close and tight.

I'll teach you how to sing a song
about the stars at night.

There are so many things to learn.
The world is all brand-new.

I'll teach you how to laugh out loud,
and kiss and cuddle too.

The more you reach, the more you learn.
There's so much here to see.
The world has wonders waiting
for your curiosity.

One day soon, you'll get so big,
I'll hold you on my hip.
You'll reach for foods you've never seen
and take new bites and sips.

You'll reach for things to balance
and wobble as you walk.

I'll teach you words like "universe"
as you begin to talk.

Reach for your hat and glasses too.
We'll take a stroll outside.
Don't worry, love, I'll do the work.
You just enjoy the ride.

Reach for the clouds up in the sky.
See how it's so blue?
I'll teach you how that pretty light
came from the sun to you.

The more you reach, the more you learn.

There's so much here to see.

The world has wonders waiting.

Come explore with me.

One day soon, you'll get so big,
I'll hold you by the hand.
You'll feel the big blue ocean,
reaching toes deep in the sand.

You'll reach for your boogie board
and catch a wave or two.

I'll teach you how the lunar pull
made those tides for you.

EARTH   MOON

Reach out for little special rocks,
collect them one by one.

I'll teach you how each one was made
when we decide we're done.

At night, we'll lie down on the ground
and look up really far.
I'll teach you how the asteroids
become our shooting stars.

Reach out for your telescope
to see the moon so bright.
I'll teach you how that big full moon
reflects the solar light.

The more you reach, the more you learn.
There's so much here to see.
The world has wonders waiting.
What will you grow up to be?

I'll teach you how to reach for things
that are very hard to do.

You may succeed, and that is great, but failing's common too.
We try and fail, jump and fall, and tumble, trip, and then
reach for my hand, I'll pull you up
and we will try again.

For being brave does not mean
That nothing makes you scared.
It means you never let your fear
prevent the dreams you've dared.

One day soon, you'll get so big,
you'll want to be with friends.
And just because you're not with me,
that's not where your reach ends.

Reach out to friends when you need help
and they'll reach out to you.
You can work together
and help those with less than you.

And when deciding what to be,
you must reach for the stars.
You could be the president
or an astronaut on Mars.

The more you reach, the more you learn.
There's so much here to see.
The world has wonders waiting—
oh, the possibilities!

One day soon, you'll get so big,
you may move far away.
Reach out to me, because you know,
I'll miss you every day.

Expand your reach throughout the globe
to cities all around.
Take risks and do the scary things.
That's where stories will be found.

Reach out for all important things
or no big thing at all.
When I have nothing left to teach,
I hope that you'll still call.

The more you reach, the more you learn.
There's so much here to do.
Spread your wings, reach for the stars—
adventure waits for you!